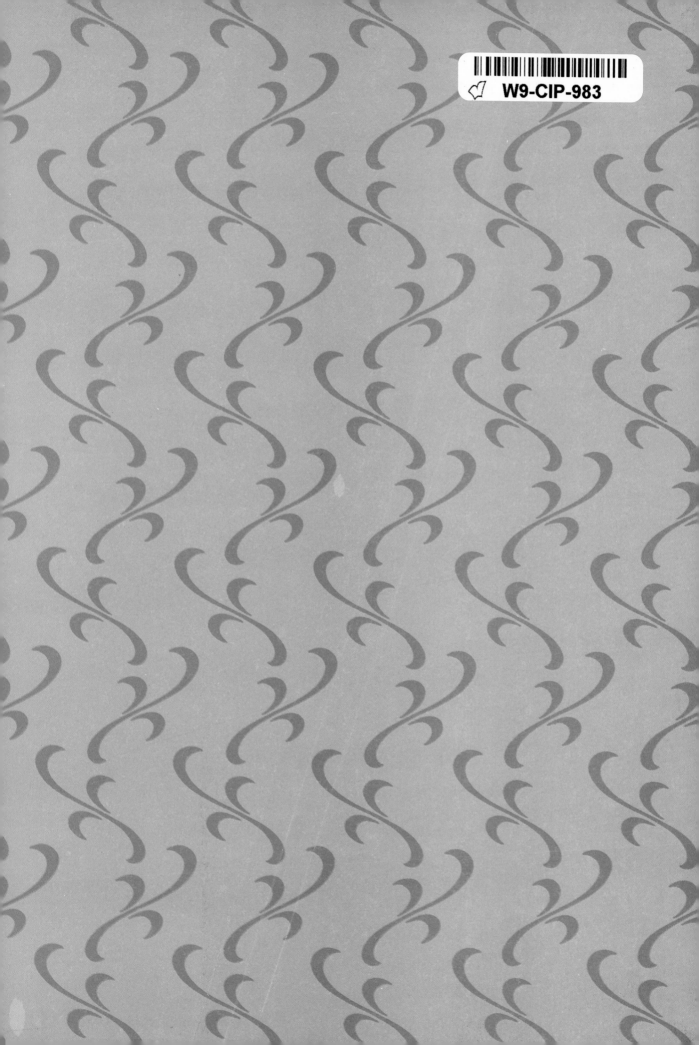

CHERISHED FAIRY TALES

THE
Velveteen Rabbit

by Margery Williams
retold by Joanne Barkan
illustrated by Jim Talbot

"Look!" said the Boy. "There's a velveteen rabbit in my Christmas stocking!"

And so there was. The toy rabbit had a soft, brown coat. He had thread whiskers and long ears lined with pink satin. The Boy loved this new toy and played with him. But after a few hours everyone sat down to a big Christmas dinner, and the Velveteen Rabbit was completely forgotten.

"Into the toy cupboard you go," said Nana, the Boy's governess, as she scooped up the Velveteen Rabbit and carried him to the nursery. She plopped him down next to an old leather horse, and there the Rabbit stayed with all the other forgotten toys.

Most of the toys in the nursery paid no attention to the shy little Rabbit. Only the wise Leather Horse was kind to him and told him all about the wonderful world of toys.

"Shall I tell you about becoming *real*?" the Leather Horse asked one evening. When the Rabbit nodded, the Horse began: "If a child truly loves you for a long, long time, then you become *real*.

Of course, by the time it happens, you will have been hugged so much that you will be quite shabby."

"Are you *real*?" asked the Velveteen Rabbit.

The Horse's eyes sparkled. "Oh, yes," he whispered with joy.

The Velveteen Rabbit thought about what the Horse had said. And the more he thought, the more he wanted to be *real*, too.

"Where is my Scotty dog?" the Boy asked one night. "I can't fall asleep without my Scotty dog!"

Nana looked at the Boy in his bed and sighed. Then she reached into the toy cupboard and pulled out the Velveteen Rabbit. "Try sleeping with this Bunny," she said.

The Boy fell asleep with the Velveteen Rabbit in his arms that night — and every night after that. When the lights were out, the Boy would tell the Rabbit stories. The Boy would build deep burrows in the blankets that he said were just like the burrows real rabbits lived in.

During the day, the Boy took the Velveteen Rabbit for picnics in the garden.

"We are the very best of friends now," the Boy said to the Rabbit.

The Velveteen Rabbit was happy — so wonderfully happy that he never noticed that his velveteen coat had been rubbed smooth and his pink satin ears had lost their shine. He had become quite shabby from all the Boy's hugs and kisses.

One spring evening, Nana called the Boy into the house for an early supper. The Velveteen Rabbit was left behind in the garden until long after sunset. When Nana and the Boy finally came to get him, Nana was a little cross.

"Imagine making such a fuss over a toy!" she said. "He's *not* a toy!" the Boy answered. "He's *real*!"

The Rabbit felt his heart fill with love. What the old Leather Horse had told him was true. He was *real* at last.

One day the Velveteen Rabbit sat quietly in the woods. The Boy had gone to pick wildflowers. The Rabbit was enjoying the sun when he noticed two furry creatures nearby. They appeared to be rabbits too, but their seams didn't show. And what was even stranger, they moved by themselves and changed shape as they hopped around.

These furry rabbits suddenly hopped up to the Velveteen Rabbit, sniffing him with their quivering noses.

"He doesn't smell right!" they exclaimed. "He isn't a real rabbit like us!"

"I *am real*!" cried the toy Rabbit. "The Boy says so!"

But the furry rabbits didn't listen. They leapt into the air and hopped away. The Velveteen Rabbit watched them. Oh, how he wished he could hop and leap the way they did.

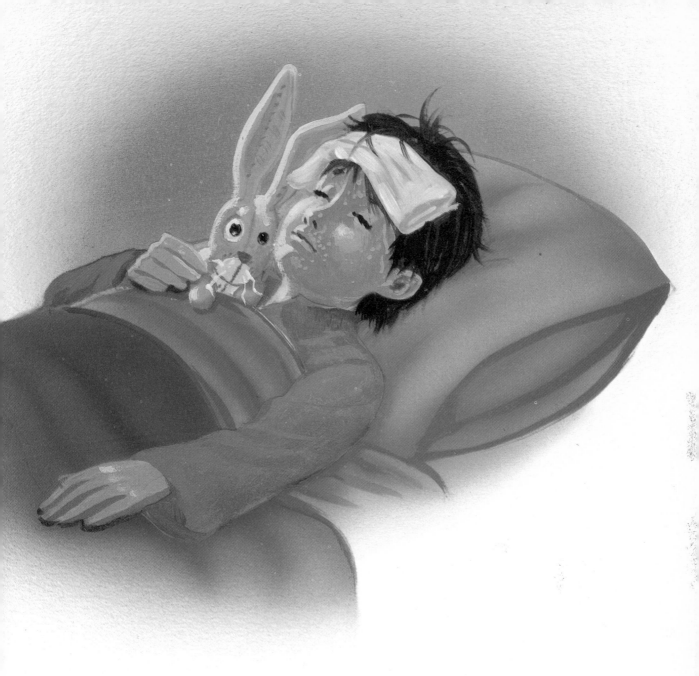

One night, the Boy fell ill. His fever climbed so high that the Velveteen Rabbit, nestled in the Boy's arms, could feel the burning heat. For many days and nights, doctors and nurses came to take care of the Boy. The Rabbit hid from view under the bedsheets so no one would take him away. He knew the Boy needed him more than ever.

Finally, one afternoon, the Boy was well enough to be carried onto the porch to enjoy the fresh air.

"Now," said the doctor, "we must clean the nursery. All the toys must be burned. They are covered with germs."

Nana collected the Boy's playthings, including the Velveteen Rabbit, and placed them in a large bag. She carried them out to the garden so that the gardener would burn them the next day.

As the sun set, the Velveteen Rabbit poked his small head out of the bag and looked around. The garden reminded him of all the happy times he and the Boy had shared. He thought of how much he loved the Boy and how much the Boy loved him. And now it would end. A real tear trickled down his shabby little nose and fell to the ground.

Ping! Suddenly, from that spot on the ground sprang a lovely fairy who gathered the Rabbit up in her arms.

"I am the Toy Fairy," she said, kissing him gently. "When well-loved toys are not needed by their children anymore, I make them *real*. Before, you were *real* only to the Boy. Now you will be *real* to everyone."

A year passed, and one day the Boy was playing in the woods when a furry rabbit hopped right up to him. The Boy stared at the rabbit and thought, "How strange! He looks like my dear old Rabbit that was lost when I was sick."

The rabbit looked at the Boy thoughtfully and then leapt into the air and hopped away. The Boy never knew that it really was his own Rabbit, the Velveteen Rabbit that he had helped become *real*.